The Golem

The Golem

Isaac Bashevis Singer

Illustrations by Uri Shulevitz

Farrar · Straus · Giroux

New York

Library of Congress catalog card no.: 82-12028
Published simultaneously in Canada by
McGraw-Hill Ryerson Ltd., Toronto
Printed in the United States of America
Designed by Cynthia Krupat
Second printing, 1983

I dedicate this book to
the persecuted and oppressed everywhere,
old and young, Jew and Gentile,
in the hope against hope that the time
of false accusations and malicious decrees
will cease one day.

I. B. S.

To Rena and Dr. Alex Messer

U. S.

Author's Note

I published the story of The Golem *in the* Jewish Daily Forward *in 1969. In the autumn of 1981 I worked on the translation, and in the process I made many changes, as I always do. I received good advice about the use of English words and expressions from my beloved wife Alma, as well as from my secretary Deborah Menashe, to whom I dictated this work. The whole text was edited by my good friend Robert Giroux, who has been my editor for twenty-two years.*

The Golem

In the time when the famous Cabbalist Rabbi Leib served as rabbi in the old city of Prague, the Jews suffered persecution. The Emperor Rudolf II, an erudite man, was intolerant of anybody outside the Catholic faith. He persecuted Protestants, and even more so the Jews, who were often accused of using Christian blood to bake Passover matzohs. Almost everybody knew that this accusation was false, that the Jewish religion forbade the eating of animal blood, let alone human. But every few years this charge was renewed. Whenever a Christian child disappeared, the enemies of the Jews immediately proclaimed that it had been killed to provide blood for matzohs. There was never a lack of false witnesses. Innocent men were executed, and it happened more than once that the lost child was later found alive and healthy.

Rabbi Leib, a great Talmudic scholar, was steeped in mysticism and magic. He seemed to have the power to cure the sick by conjuring up supernatural forces and by using various cameos and talismans. Whenever an innocent member of his congregation was imprisoned, Rabbi Leib hastened to prove the man's innocence. Many believed that Rabbi Leib could call on the help of angels and even demons and hobgoblins in times of great danger to his community.

In Prague there lived a squire by the name of Count Jan Bratislawski who had been immensely rich, with many estates and hundreds of serfs, but he had lost his fortune in gambling, drinking, and private wars with other landlords. His wife felt so disgraced by his bad behavior that she fell ill and died. She left him a little daughter, Hanka.

At the same time there lived in Prague a Jew by the name of Reb Eliezer Polner. He was an able and diligent businessman, and although he lived in the ghetto he became a well-known banker, not only in Prague but throughout the whole of Europe. Reb Eliezer was also known for his charity in helping both Jews and Christians. He was nearing sixty and had a silver-white beard. Even on weekdays, he wore a sable hat and a long silk coat with a broad sash. Reb Eliezer had a large house, married sons and daughters, and a bevy of grandchildren. He was a scholar in his own way. It was his custom to get up at sunrise every day and pray and study the Bible and the Talmud until noon. Only then did he go to the bank to conduct his business. His wife, Sheindel, came from a distinguished family and was as God-fearing and as goodhearted as her husband. Daily she visited the poorhouse, bringing bread and hot soup to the poor and sick.

Since Count Bratislawski was always in need of money, he had to sell most of his fields and forests and also his serfs, who were then, at the end of the sixteenth century, bought and sold like cattle. He owed Reb Eliezer's bank a lot of money, and eventually Reb Eliezer had to refuse him further loans.

In that year, in the month of March, which fell

around the Jewish month of Nissan, the Count had been playing cards with a group of rich gamblers every day of the week and late into the night. He had lost all the gold ducats he had in his purse. He was eager to win his money back, and began to play on credit, signing a note that he would repay within three days any debt that he might incur. To break a promise like that was considered a terrible disgrace among these gamblers. It happened more than once that a gambler who could not repay his debt shot himself with his pistol.

After Count Bratislawski had signed this note, he continued to play cards with great fervor, all the while drinking wine and smoking tobacco. By the time the game had finally ended, Count Bratislawski had lost seventy-five thousand ducats. He was too drunk to grasp what he had done. He went back to his castle and slept for many hours. Only when he awoke did he realize what had happened. He didn't possess even seventy-five ducats. All his properties had been sold or mortgaged.

When the Count's wife, Helena, died, she left to her little girl, Hanka, a great amount of jewelry worth over a million ducats. This inheritance was held in the custody of the court because Count Bratislawski could not be trusted to hold on to these valuables. According to her mother's will, Hanka was to inherit the jewels at the age of eighteen.

When Bratislawski sobered up, he fell into deep despair. He loved life too much to commit suicide. Even though he knew that Reb Eliezer could not grant him credit any more, he asked his coachman to harness his carriage and take him to Reb Eliezer's bank in the ghetto. When the Count mentioned the sum that he would like to borrow, Reb Eliezer said, "Your Highness, you know very well that you could never repay a debt like that."

"I must have the money!" Bratislawski shouted.

"I'm sorry, but you cannot get it from my bank," Reb Eliezer answered calmly.

"You cursed Jew! I will get the money one way or another," the Count screamed in rage. "And you will pay dearly for your insolence in refusing a loan to the great Count Bratislawski."

Saying these words, the Count spat into Reb Eliezer's face. Reb Eliezer humbly wiped off the spittle with his kerchief and said, "Forgive me, Count, but there was no sense in gambling for such high stakes and signing notes that cannot be honored."

"Be sure I will get the money, while you will rot in prison and be hanged. Remember my words."

"Life and death are in God's hands," Reb Eliezer said. "If I am destined to die, I will accept God's decree with humility."

Count Bratislawski left and went back to his castle to ponder a way out of his dilemma. He was greedy for two things: money to cover his debts, and revenge on the Jew. He soon devised a devilish plan.

Since it was only two weeks to Passover, the Jews in Prague were busy baking matzohs. The winter had been unusually cold, but the month of Nissan brought the warm breezes of spring. It was Reb Eliezer's custom to study Mishnah, the code of Jewish law, at night before going to bed. This time he had chosen the section that dealt with the laws pertaining to the baking of matzohs, preparing of the Seder, reciting of the Haggadah, and drinking of four goblets of sanctified wine. Even though more than three thousand years have passed since the exodus from Egypt, the Jews, all over the world, have never forgotten that they were slaves to Pharaoh, the ruler of the Egyptians, and that God granted them freedom.

Suddenly Reb Eliezer heard heavy steps and then a brutal knocking at the door. The maids and male servants were asleep. Reb Eliezer opened the door himself and saw a group of soldiers holding their naked swords in their hands. Their leader, a corporal, asked, "Are you the Jew Eliezer Polner?"

"Yes, I am."

"Chain him and take him away," the corporal said.

"Why? What wrong have I done?" Reb Eliezer asked in perplexity.

"This they will tell you later. Meanwhile, let's go."

Reb Eliezer spent that night in jail. The next morning they brought him to an investigator's chamber. It was where the most dangerous criminals were brought. There Reb Eliezer saw Count Bratislawski and some others—among them, a man who looked like a drunk and a woman whose face was full of warts and who squinted. The investigator said, "Jew, you are accused of breaking into the house of our noble Count Bratislawski and taking away his little daughter, Hanka, by force with the purpose of killing her and using her blood for matzohs."

Reb Eliezer went white in the face. "I have never had the privilege of visiting the Count's castle," he said in a choked voice. "I spend every night in my house. My wife, my children, my sons-in-law, my daughters-in-law, and all my servants can testify that I'm telling the truth."

"All those people are Jews," the investigator said. "But there are two Christian witnesses who saw you break into the Count's castle and drag away his child in a sack."

"Witnesses? What witnesses?"

"Here are the witnesses." The investigator pointed to the drunken man and the woman with warts on her face. "Tell what you have seen. You, Stefan, speak first."

Stefan seemed benumbed from drinking, even though it was yet morning. He shuffled his feet and stuttered: "Yesterday night, I mean the day before yesterday, no, it was three days back, I heard a noise in Hanka's room. I lit a candle and looked in. There stood this Jew with a knife in one hand and a sack in the other. He pushed Hanka into the sack and went away. I heard him mumble to himself, 'Her red-hot blood will be just right for our matzohs.' "

"How could you let me take away the Count's child without defending her and rousing everybody in the castle?" Reb Eliezer asked in a shaking voice. "You are younger and stronger than I am."

Stefan's mouth dropped open. His tongue lolled. His bulging eyes rolled over in his head. His feet faltered, and he held on to the wall. "You, Jew, threatened me with your knife."

"Your Honor, don't you see that it is all a shameless lie?" Reb Eliezer said. "First of all, the Jews never use blood for any purpose whatsoever. Second, according to the Mosaic law, nothing can be used in the baking of matzohs except flour and water. And then why should I, a man of sixty, a banker, a leader of the congregation, commit an abomination like that? Even madness must have some logic."

"Barbara was there, and she saw it too," Stefan said.

"What did you see, Barbara?" the investigator asked.

The woman squinted. "I saw the Jew. I opened the door and I saw him push Hanka into the sack."

"And you didn't call for help?" Reb Eliezer asked.

"I, too, was afraid of your knife."

"Why didn't you call for help later?" Reb Eliezer asked.

"I don't need to answer to you, you vicious murderer!" Barbara screeched, threatening Reb Eliezer with her fist.

"Your honor, Count Bratislawski came to me a short time ago and asked me for the loan of a huge sum of money," Reb Eliezer said. "I had to refuse him since he already owes me and others a lot of money that he cannot repay. He then warned me that I would rot in prison. He is now trying to revenge himself on me."

"It is all one big lie!" the Count cried out. "I never asked him to lend me any money. The Jew Eliezer is nothing but a cold-blooded killer, and he should be tortured and hanged, together with all those who helped him commit this heinous crime."

"Your Honor—" Reb Eliezer began to speak.

"Silence, Jew! There are two witnesses who testify that you committed the crime, and this is enough. You had better confess whom you conspired with in this horrible offense. If you try to deny it, we have plenty of means to drag the truth out of your mouth, you merciless murderer," the investigator growled.

"God in heaven, I didn't plan anything with anybody. I never leave the house at night, because I am an elderly man and I don't see well in the dark. I am as capable of taking a child out of its bed and doing the things you accuse me of as walking on my head. I implore Your Honor to think over what an absurdity this condemnation is, how wild, how preposterous, how cruel—"

"There's nothing to think over. Who waited for you and the child you captured outside? Where did you take her? How did you cut off her young life?" the investigator asked.

"All I can say is that I stayed home that night just as I do every other night. I haven't done anything wrong."

"The old Jewish stubbornness," Count Bratislawski cried out. "They are caught red-handed and they still attempt to deny the truth. You will hang, Jew! And even your God will not be able to save you."

"You can say whatever you want, sir, about me, but don't blaspheme God. He can help us, if we deserve it."

"Well? Why doesn't he break your chains?" Bratislawski mocked. "Why doesn't he send down thunder to strike me dead?"

"You, sir, don't need to advise God what to do," Reb Eliezer said.

"I order the Jew Eliezer Polner to be kept in

prison on bread and water and to be tortured until he reveals what he did with that helpless child and who assisted him in this abhorrence," the investigator said.

Immediately, the soldiers led Reb Eliezer Polner out and threw him back into jail. The two witnesses, Stefan and Barbara, were also led out of the investigator's chamber. Count Bratislawski winked to them and smirked.

When Bratislawski was finally alone with the investigator, he said, "Now that Hanka's death has been verified, I, her only heir, should be able to receive her entire fortune without delay."

"Wait awhile," the investigator replied. "Let the whole scandal blow over first. This particular Jew has many friends even among the Christians. Hardly anyone would believe that this old banker came in the middle of the night with a sack to snatch away your little daughter. The case may later be appealed to a higher court. The Jew may even have some allies in the Emperor's palace. As long as the Jew is alive and has not yet confessed, he cannot be hanged. You will have to wait for Hanka's estate."

"I cannot wait. My honor is at stake," Bratislawski said. "If I don't pay my debt immediately, my name is ruined forever."

The investigator smiled cunningly. "Your name was ruined when you were born."

"My name will stay pure and among the best in all of Bohemia," Bratislawski boasted.

"Well, time will tell."

Bratislawski and the investigator continued to converse and to whisper for a long time. Even though they called themselves Christians, neither of them believed in God and in His commandments. Money, cards, wine, hazardous games, all kinds of idle pleasures were the essence of their lives.

More than all the other Jews in Prague, Rabbi Leib was heartbroken when he heard the terrible news of Reb Eliezer's arrest. All his life Rabbi Leib had waited for the coming of the Messiah, when the world would be redeemed from all suffering and iniquity, and God's light would fill each soul, each heart. Even the carnivorous beasts would cease devouring other animals, and a wolf would dwell peacefully with a lamb. God would bring back His people to the Holy Land, the Holy Temple would be rebuilt in Jerusalem, and there would be a resurrection of the dead.

Instead, such an ugly accusation directed toward one of the most honest men of the congregation! The rabbi knew that a succession of arrests would follow and the hangman of Prague would soon be preparing the gallows and the rope for an execution.

Exactly at twelve o'clock at night, Rabbi Leib rose for his midnight prayers. As usual, he put ashes on his head and began his lamentations over the destruction of the Temple in ancient times. He also shed tears over the misfortune that had befallen Reb Eliezer Polner and the whole Jewish community at the present time.

Suddenly the door opened and a little man entered wearing a patched robe, with a rope around his loins and with a sack on his back like a beggar. Rabbi Leib was surprised. He thought he had chained the door before beginning his prayers, but it seemed the door was open. Rabbi Leib interrupted his prayers and extended his hand to the stranger, since honoring guests is even more important in the eyes of God than prayer. Rabbi Leib greeted the man with the words *Sholom Aleichem,* "Peace be with you," and asked him, "What can I do for you?"

"Thank you, I don't need anything. I shall leave soon," the stranger said.

"In the middle of the night?" Rabbi Leib asked.

"I must take my leave soon."

Rabbi Leib looked at the man, and at that moment it became clear to him that this was not a usual wanderer. Rabbi Leib saw in his eyes something which only great men possess and which only great men recognize—a mixture of love, dignity, and fear of God. Rabbi Leib realized that the stranger might be one of the thirty-six hidden saints through whose merit the world existed, according to tradition. Never before had Rabbi Leib had the privilege of meeting a man of this stature. Rabbi Leib bowed his head and said, "Honored guest, we here in Prague are in great distress. Our enemies are about to de-

stroy us. We are sinking up to our very necks in tribulations."

"I know," the stranger answered.

"What should we do?"

"Make a golem and he will save you."

"A golem? How? From what?"

"From clay. You will engrave one of God's names on the golem's forehead, and with the power of that Sacred Name he will live for a time and do his mission. His name will be Joseph. But take care that he should not fall into the follies of flesh and blood."

"What Sacred Name shall I engrave?" Rabbi Leib asked.

The stranger took out from his breast pocket a piece of chalk and on the cover of Rabbi Leib's prayer book wrote down some Hebrew letters. Then he said, "I must go now. See to it that all this remains a secret. And employ the golem only to help the Jews."

Before Rabbi Leib was able to utter a word of gratitude, the man vanished. Only then did the rabbi realize that the door had been chained all along. The rabbi stood there trembling, and praising God for sending him that heavenly messenger.

Although the holy man had told Rabbi Leib that his appearance and the making of the golem must remain a secret, Rabbi Leib realized that he had to share it with his beadle, Todrus. Todrus had served Rabbi Leib for the last forty years, and he had kept many secrets. A strong man, he was totally devoted to the rabbi. He had neither a wife nor children. Serving Rabbi Leib was his entire life; he lived in the rabbi's house and made his bed next to Rabbi Leib's chamber of study, so that he should always be ready to serve him even in the middle of the night. Rabbi Leib knocked lightly at his door and whispered, "Todrus."

"Rabbi, what is it that you wish?" Todrus asked, awaking immediately.

"I need clay."

Another person would have asked, "Clay? At this late hour?" But Todrus had learned not to question the rabbi's commands. "How much clay?" he asked.

"A lot of it."

"A sackful?"

"At least ten sackfuls."

"Where should I put all this clay?"

"In the attic of the synagogue."

There was wonder in Todrus's eyes, but all he said was, "Yes, Rabbi."

"The whole thing must remain a secret, even from my family," Rabbi Leib said.

"So be it," Todrus said, and he left.

Rabbi Leib continued his prayers. He could be certain that Todrus would do as he was told.

After finishing his night prayers, Rabbi Leib went back to sleep, and he woke up at sunrise.

Rabbi Leib knew quite well the meaning of the word *golem*. There were legends among the Jews about golems who were created by ancient saints to save them in a time of great danger. According to the legends, only the most saintly rabbis were given this power, and only after many days of supplication, fasting, and indulging in the mysteries of the Cabbalah. It never occurred to the modest Rabbi Leib that a man like himself would be granted this privilege. "Could it be that I dreamed it?" Rabbi Leib asked himself. But early in the morning, when he opened the door to the synagogue, he saw traces of clay on the floor. While Rabbi Leib slept, Todrus had gone out to the clay ditches in the suburbs of Prague and brought the clay to the attic. One had to be unusually strong and devoted to accomplish all this between midnight and sunrise.

It would have been impossible for Rabbi Leib to climb up to the attic without the knowledge of his family and stay there for many hours. Luckily, the rabbi's wife, Genendel, had to attend a wedding that day, and she took her children and her maid with her. The bride was a distant relative of Genendel, an orphan, and the wedding took place in a nearby village. Rabbi Leib was not obligated to officiate at the ceremony.

In the attic, Rabbi Leib found the sacks with the clay and began to sculpt the figure of a man. Rabbi Leib did not use a chisel but his fingers to carve the figure of the golem. He kneaded the clay like dough. He was working with great speed; at the same time he prayed for success in what he was doing. All day Rabbi Leib was busy in the attic, and when it was time for the evening prayer, a large shape of a man with a huge head, broad shoulders, and enormous hands and feet was lying on the floor—a clay giant. The rabbi looked at him in astonishment. He could never have mastered this without the help of Almighty and Special Providence. The rabbi had taken with him the prayer book in which his saintly visitor had written down the name of God. Rabbi Leib engraved it on the forehead of the golem in such small letters that only he himself could distinguish the Hebrew characters. Immediately, the clay figure started to show signs of life.

The golem began to move his arms and legs and tried to lift his head. However, the rabbi had been careful not to engrave the entire Sacred Name. He left out a small part of the last letter, which was an Aleph, so that the golem should not begin to act before he was dressed in garments. Since the rabbi knew that the people of the community would wonder why he was not at the synagogue for the evening prayers, he decided to leave the golem unfinished where he was and began to climb down the narrow steps. Just then Todrus the beadle came in from the street, and the rabbi said to him, "Todrus, holy spirits have helped me to make a golem to defend the Jews of Prague. Climb up to the attic and see for yourself. But the golem needs to be dressed, and you will have to take his measurements and find clothes for him. I'm going to the evening prayers, and when you find the clothes, come and let me know."

"Yes, Rabbi."

Rabbi Leib went to pray, and Todrus climbed up the spiral stairs to the attic. Outside, the sun was setting, and by the light from crevices in the roof Todrus saw the golem lying on the floor and trying to get up. A terrible fear came over Todrus. Like many other Jews in Prague, he had heard stories about golems, but he never believed that the actual creation of one could take place in his time and almost before his very eyes.

For a long time Todrus stood there motionless. "Where will I get clothes for a giant like this?" he thought in consternation. Even if a tailor could be found to take the golem's measurements and sew a robe and trousers for him, and a shoemaker could be assigned to make a pair of boots for him, it would take weeks or even months—while the Jews of Prague were in great peril right now.

Todrus knew from forty years of service that when Rabbi Leib gave an order, he must act without delay. The sun had set and it became dark in the attic. Todrus rushed down the stairs, his heart pounding and his legs buckling under him. He went out into the street and took a deep breath. He then began to walk in the direction of the old marketplace, hoping against hope to find some miraculous solution. Night had fallen and the stores began to close. Suddenly Todrus saw in a store a huge hat that was too big to fit any human head. It was a hatmaker's window sample. When Todrus entered the store he saw a robe, a pair of pants, and shoes of the same unbelievable size. Amazed, he asked the owner where he had obtained these curious things. The owner told him that forty years ago a foreign circus had come to Prague and performed a play called *David and Goliath*. It so happened that the circus people had quarreled among themselves, the play had failed to attract a public, and all the props and sets were sold for a very small price. The proprietor of the store said to Todrus: "I got these things for a pittance and I bought them just as a rarity that might attract customers. However, they have been here for so many years that no one looks at them any more. Also, they are covered with dust and I have neither the time nor the patience to air them or brush them. Why do you ask? I'm about to close the store for the night."

"I want to buy them," Todrus said. "If you sell them to me at a reasonable price."

"What are you going to do with them?"

"Who knows?" Todrus replied. "Just give me a reasonable price."

"Well, this is the strangest thing that has happened to me in all these years," the storekeeper said. "No one has ever shown any interest in these paraphernalia." He gave Todrus an exceptionally low offer, and in a matter of minutes the deal was completed. Todrus was known for his honesty, and he always carried a purse with money that belonged to the community and that Rabbi Leib entrusted to him.

Todrus feared that people in the street might stop him in wonderment, but luckily no one was outside at this time of night. The men were all in the synagogue, and the women were preparing dinner for their husbands and children. Todrus managed to climb the stairs of the synagogue attic without being seen and put down the garments, the hat, and the shoes for the golem. How strange, the golem had managed to sit up! A half-moon was shining outside, and it allowed Todrus to see the golem sitting, leaning on an old barrel with mildewed books, and looking at him in bewilderment. Todrus was seized with such fright that he intoned the words "Hear, O Israel, the Lord is our God, the Lord is One."

After some time he heard Rabbi Leib coming up the stairs with a lantern in which a wax candle was burning. The rabbi saw the robe, the hat, and the shoes and said to Todrus, "Everything is planned by Providence. Even though man has free will, Providence foresees all the decisions man would make." After they dressed the golem in these bizarre clothes, the rabbi said: "Thank you, Todrus, and leave me alone now."

"Yes, Rabbi," Todrus said, and he descended as quickly as he could.

For a long while Rabbi Leib gaped at the golem, perplexed by his own creation. How strange the synagogue attic looked in the dim light of the lantern! In the corners, huge spiderwebs hung from the rafters. On the floor lay old and torn prayer shawls, cracked ram's-horns, broken candelabra, parts of candlesticks, Hanukkah lamps, as well as faded pages of manuscripts written by unknown or forgotten scribes. Through the crevices and holes in the roof the moonlit dust reflected the colors of the rainbow. One could sense the spirits of generations who had lived, suffered, served God, withstood both persecution and temptation, and become silent forever. A strange thought ran through Rabbi Leib's mind: "If those who deny that God created the world could witness what I, a man born from the womb of a woman, have done, they would be ashamed of their heresy. However, such is the power of Satan that he can blind people's eyes and confuse their minds. Satan, too, was created by God so that man should have free will to choose between good and evil."

As Rabbi Leib stood there looking at the golem, the golem seemed to look back at him with his clay

eyes. Then the rabbi said, "Golem, you have not been completely formed, but I am about to finish you now. Let it be known to you that you were created for a short time and for a purpose. Don't ever try to stray from this path. You will do as I will tell you."

Saying these words, Rabbi Leib finished engraving the letter Aleph. Immediately the golem began to rise. The rabbi said to him, "Walk down and wait for me in the yard of the synagogue for further instructions."

"Yes," the golem said in a hollow voice, as if it rose from a cave. Then he walked down to the synagogue courtyard, which was empty. The people of the ghetto went to sleep early and woke up at sunrise. After the prayer services, everybody had gone home.

Rabbi Leib's mind was too occupied with the golem to pay much attention to the conversation of his wife and children, who had returned from the wedding and were talking about the bride, the bridegroom, and the guests. Usually, the rabbi went to sleep early, so he could get up for the midnight prayers. This time he waited until his wife and children went to sleep, and then he went out silently to the synagogue courtyard. The golem was standing there waiting. The rabbi approached him. "Golem, your name will be Joseph from now on."

"Yes."

"Joseph, soon you will have to find the daughter of Count Bratislawski, a little girl by the name of Hanka. Her father maintains that the Jews have killed her, but I am sure that he is hiding her somewhere. Don't ask me where to find her. Those powers that gave you life will also give you the knowledge of where she is. You are part of the earth, and the earth knows many things—how to grow grass, flowers, wheat, rye, fruit. Wait for the day when Reb Eliezer is brought to trial, and then bring the girl and show our enemies how false their accusation was."

"Yes."

"Is there anything you want to ask?" the rabbi said to the golem.

"What ask?" answered the golem.

"Since you were created for a single purpose, you were given a different brain from that of a man. However, one never knows how a brain works. While you rest and wait for the day when you will have to find Hanka, you may sleep, you may dream, you may see things or hear voices. Perhaps demons may try to attach themselves to you. Don't pay any attention to them. Nothing evil can befall you. The people of Prague are not to see you until the day you have to be seen. Until then, go back to the attic where I formed you and sleep there the peaceful sleep of clay. Good night."

Rabbi Leib turned his face toward his home. He knew the golem would do exactly as he was told. When he reached home, the rabbi recited the night prayer and went to bed. For the first time in many years he could not fall asleep. A great power was granted to him from heaven, and he was afraid that he had not deserved it. He also felt a kind of compassion for the golem. The rabbi thought he saw an expression of perplexity in the golem's eyes. It seemed to the rabbi that his eyes were asking, "Who am I? Why am I here? What is the secret of my being?" Rabbi Leib often saw the same bewilderment in the eyes of newborn children and even in the eyes of animals.

Those who wanted the Jews to have a miserable Passover had arranged for the trial to take place shortly. The day before Passover, Reb Eliezer Polner was brought to court, together with a number of community leaders who were supposed to have assisted him in the murder.

Three judges sat with perukes on their heads, dressed in long black togas. The Jews stood bound in chains, guarded by soldiers carrying swords and spears. The chief judge had forbidden the Jews of Prague to witness the trial, but quite a few enemies of Israel came with their wives and daughters to see the disgrace of the Jews. The prosecutor pointed his index finger at Reb Eliezer Polner and the other accused Jews, and said, "They consider themselves God's chosen people, but see how they conduct themselves. Instead of being grateful to our Emperor and to all of us for allowing them to live here, they slaughter our children and pour their blood into their matzohs. They are not God's people but followers of the Devil. The blood of the murdered little Hanka is calling for vengeance. Not only the Jew Eliezer Polner and the other conspirators but the whole Jewish community is guilty."

A number of old women began to sob when they heard these words. Some of the young ones winked and smiled. They understood that the whole thing was contrived. Count Bratislawski pretended he was wiping away his tears. The Jews had called Rabbi Leib as a witness for the defense, and the prosecutor asked him, "Is it written in your cursed Talmud that Christian blood should be poured into the dough of your matzohs?"

"There is not a trace of it, either in the Talmud or in any other of our Sacred Books," Rabbi Leib answered. "We don't bake our matzohs in dark cellars but in bakeries, with the doors open. Anyone can come and see. The matzohs consist of flour and water only."

"Isn't it a fact that hundreds of Jews have been condemned for using blood in matzohs?" the prosecutor asked.

"I'm sorry to say that this is true. But this does not prove that the accused were guilty. There is never a lack of wicked witnesses who are ready to testify falsely, especially if they are bribed to do so."

"Isn't it a fact that many of those Jews confessed their crime?"

"This, too, is true, but they confessed after their bodies were broken on a torture wheel and after their fingers and toes were pricked with glowing needles. There is a limit to how much pain a man can endure. You have all heard the case of the town of Altona, of an innocent Christian woman who was accused of being a witch and was tortured for so long that she confessed she had sold her soul to Satan, and was burned at the stake. Later it was revealed that an enemy of this woman hired evil men and women to bear witness against her."

The chief judge pounded his gavel on the desk and said, "Answer the prosecutor's questions and don't talk about matters that are irrelevant to this trial. We are here to judge the murder of a child, not the innocence of a witch."

Suddenly the locked door of the courthouse burst open, and a giant with a clay-yellow face rushed in with a little girl in his huge arms. The little girl was weeping, and the giant put her down near the witness stand, then left immediately. Everything took place so quickly that the people in the courthouse could barely realize what was happening. No one could utter a word. The little girl ran to Count Bratislawski, clutched his legs, and screamed, "Papa, Papa!"

Jan Bratislawski became as white as chalk. The witnesses who were supposed to proceed at the stand stood there open-mouthed. The astonished prosecutor lifted his arms with an expression of despair. Some of the women in the courthouse began to laugh, while others sobbed hysterically. The chief judge shook his bewigged head and asked, "Who are you, little girl? What is your name?"

"My name is Hanka. This is my papa," the crying girl managed to answer, pointing her little finger at Jan Bratislawski.

"Is this your daughter, Hanka?" the judge asked.

Bratislawski did not answer.

"Who is the giant who brought you here?" the judge asked. "Where have you been, Hanka, all these days?"

"Be silent, don't say a word!" Bratislawski shouted to his daughter.

"Answer, where were you?" the judge insisted.

"In our house, in a cellar," the girl answered.

"Who put you there?" the judge asked.

"Keep quiet. Don't say a word," Bratislawski admonished his daughter.

"You must answer, this is the law," the judge said. "Who put you into the cellar?"

Even though the judge was on the side of Count Bratislawski, he was no longer in a mood to take part in this farce. There were many Christian citizens of Prague who wanted to know the truth. The chief judge had heard that even the Emperor was irritated by this sham trial. The intelligent Christians in Europe did not believe in this horrifying accusation any more. The shrewd judge had therefore decided to play the role of an upright man.

Hanka stood there in silence, looking back and forth from the judge to her father. Then she said, "This man and this woman locked me up in the cellar," and she pointed to Stefan and Barbara. "They told me that my own papa asked them to do so."

"It's a lie. She's lying," Bratislawski protested. "The Jews have bewitched my darling daughter to believe in this nonsense. She is my only beloved child, and I would rather let my eyes be cut out than do her any harm. I'm the great Jan Bratislawski, a pillar of the state of Bohemia."

"Not any more," the chief judge said in a cold voice. "You have lost your fortune playing cards. You signed a note that you could not pay. You bribed these two ruffians to put your child into a cellar in order to inherit her jewels. For such crimes you will be punished severely and lose all titles to your lands and property. Stefan and Barbara," the judge continued, "who told you to put this tender child into the cellar? Tell the truth, or I will order you to be flogged."

"The Count did it," both of them answered.

Barbara began to scream. "He gave us drink and threatened us with death if we didn't obey him."

"He promised me twenty gold ducats and a barrel of vodka," Stefan exclaimed.

The judge pounded his gavel again and again, but the uproar in the courthouse did not stop. Some men were shouting, others shook their fists. Some women fainted. Count Bratislawski lifted up his hand and began to tell the court that the judge himself was an accomplice to his crime and was supposed to get a share of the inheritance, but the judge called out, "Soldiers, I order you to chain this foul criminal Jan Bratislawski and throw him into the dungeon." Then he pointed at Bratislawski and added: "Whatever this rascal has to say, he will say on the gallows with a noose around his neck. And now, Jews, you are all free. Go back to your homes and celebrate your holiday. Soldiers, take off their chains. In a just court such as this, and with an honorable judge like myself, the truth always prevails."

"Who was the giant?" voices asked from all sides. But no one knew the answer. It was all like a dream or one of the tales old women tell while spinning flax by candlelight.

Although the saint had told Rabbi Leib to keep the creation of the golem a secret, the fact of the golem's existence became known. In the whole city of Prague, and all over Bohemia, the news spread about the giant who saved the Jews in Prague from the false accusation. The Emperor Rudolf II also heard about the trial and ordered Rabbi Leib to bring the giant to his palace immediately after the eight days of Passover.

The night after the golem brought Hanka into the court and Reb Eliezer and the other community leaders were freed, the rabbi went up to the synagogue attic and found the golem lying there like a graven image. Rabbi Leib approached him, rubbed off the Holy Name that he had engraved on his forehead, and so made sure the golem would not appear on the days of Passover and cause a turmoil among Jews and Christians alike.

It was a happy holiday for the Jews of Prague. While they were reciting the miracles that their forefathers had known in the land of Egypt, they were also murmuring about the great miracle that had taken place right here in Prague. On Passover, every Jew is a king and every Jewess a queen. It was a great comfort to know that God was still here to protect His people from the pharaohs of today as He did more than three thousand years ago.

When Passover ended, Rabbi Leib went up to the attic in the middle of the night and, in order to fulfill the Emperor's command, again engraved the Holy Name on the golem's forehead. This time the rabbi could not hide the existence of the golem from his family or other Jews or even from the Gentiles.

When the rabbi's wife, children, and grandchildren saw the golem walking with Rabbi Leib, they screamed and ran away in panic. The horses that were harnessed to wagons and carriages began to gallop wildly or stood on their hind legs when they saw the golem. The dogs barked madly. The pigeons

flew up as high as they could and circled over the rooftops. Crows were crowing. Even the oxen and cows began to bellow when they saw the golem striding with his long legs, his head towering over everybody.

When Rabbi Leib approached the Emperor's palace and the guards saw the golem, they forgot their duty to guard the entrance to the royal manor and ran for dear life. The Emperor soon learned what was going on, and he came out to meet the rabbi and his monstrous companion. Rabbi Leib bowed his head and told the golem to do the same.

The Emperor asked, "Who is this colossus—your Messiah?"

"Your Majesty," Rabbi Leib answered, "he is not our Messiah but a golem made out of clay."

"Who gave him life? How did he come to Prague?" the Emperor asked.

Rabbi Leib could not tell the truth, but neither did he want to lie. He therefore said, "Your Majesty, there are secrets that cannot be divulged even to a king."

The conversation between the Emperor and Rabbi

Leib lasted a long while, and all this time the golem stood stiff, not moving a limb of his body. The Emperor said, "With a giant like this, you Jews could conquer the whole world. What guarantee do we have that you will not invade all the countries and make all of us into slaves?" To this Rabbi Leib replied, "We Jews have tasted slavery in the land of Egypt, and therefore we don't want to enslave others. The golem is only a temporary help to us in a time of exceptional danger. The Messiah will come when the Jews deserve to be redeemed by their virtuous deeds."

"How long is this monstrosity supposed to live?" the Emperor asked, pointing at the golem.

"Not a day longer than he is needed," Rabbi Leib answered.

While the Emperor and the rabbi conversed, the church bells all over Prague began to ring. There was a high tower in the city of Prague that was called the Tower of Five. So ancient was this tower that no one knew the reason for its peculiar name. There was a legend that it belonged to five royal brothers in the times when the people of Bohemia still worshipped idols. In the steeple at the top of the tower there was a copper bell, and a watchman was always on the lookout for fires or for sudden invasion by enemies. When the watchman saw the golem, he began to ring the bell, and the bell ringers in all the churches did the same. The Emperor became anxious and asked Rabbi Leib to dispose of the golem, but Rabbi Leib promised him that nothing evil would happen to anyone in Prague or in any place of the Holy Empire. It was the first time in the history of the Jews after they were exiled from their land that a rabbi had to promise an emperor that the rabbi would safeguard him and his people from impending mishap.

When Rabbi Leib returned to the ghetto with the golem, the city seemed empty. All the stores were closed; no one dared to come out. The city was deserted, as in a time of epidemic, when people shun the outdoors so as not to breathe the pestilent air.

Since the rabbi had promised the Emperor to do away with the golem as quickly as possible, and since no immediate danger threatened the Jews of Prague, the rabbi decided to bring the golem to the attic and erase the Holy Name. Rabbi Leib told the golem to go up to the attic and wait there for him. The golem did as Rabbi Leib said. When the alarm subsided and the leaders of the congregation came to the rabbi to ask him about his audience with the Emperor, the rabbi told them everything and assured them that tomorrow the golem would be nothing more than a huge chunk of clay. There would again be peace and order in the city of Prague, as well as in the Jewish ghetto. Some of the community leaders said to the rabbi, "Why do away with a pillar of strength for the Jews? Perhaps we should let him live." But Rabbi Leib said, "According to our Holy Books, this is not the way our salvation will come. Our Messiah will be a holy man of flesh and blood, not a gigantic clay figure." Rabbi Leib continued: "What God did for us once, He can do again in times of great peril." He quoted the saying of the Talmud: Miracles do not occur every day.

THE GOLEM

Rabbi Leib had kept his promise to the saint who visited him in the middle of the night, and he never confided to his wife, Genendel, with what power he created the golem, even though she often questioned him about it. But Genendel learned about it from Todrus the beadle. The reason Genendel wanted to know all the details of the golem was this: the rabbi's house had a garden with many fruit trees and an abundance of flowers, and in the middle of it stood a huge rock. This rock was so large that to remove it with an ax and shovel would have taken years. There was a legend about this rock: a great treasure of gold was supposed to be buried under it. According to the story, there once lived a very rich Jewish man in the city of Prague, an alchemist who could turn lead into gold. All day long he studied the Talmud and other sacred books, but at night he explored the magic of alchemy. He did not use the gold for his own comfort but gave it to the poor. He also sent gold by messengers to the Holy Land, where he supported a yeshivah for Cabbalists.

However, one day the ruler of Bohemia, a vicious and greedy tyrant, decided to kill this saint and take all his treasure for himself. He invented some meaningless crime which this alchemist was supposed to have committed, and he was sent to the gallows. As the martyr stood at the gallows with a noose around his neck, he called out to the ruler, "You will never live to see this gold or make any use of it." A minute after the holy alchemist was hanged, the ruler of the land became blind, and so he could never see his loot. He also became a leper, and the stench of his flesh was so terrible that he had to abdicate, and he was sent into a secluded area for lepers. The new ruler also wanted the gold for himself, but an immense rock fell from heaven and buried itself as well as the alchemist's gold deep in the earth where Rabbi Leib's garden was now. No amount of work could dig the treasure out.

Genendel was greatly involved in charity. For many years she had fantasies about moving the rock and taking out the gold to help the poor people in the ghetto as well as the Cabbalists in the Holy Land. Since Rabbi Leib was known as a Cabbalist himself,

Genendel often tried to persuade her husband to use the powers of the Cabbalah to remove the rock. But Rabbi Leib had told her that what heaven has covered, no man can uncover. Now that Genendel witnessed the supernatural strength of the golem, it occurred to her that destiny might have sent him to salvage the lost treasure. After Rabbi Leib returned from the audience with the Emperor, Genendel tried to convince her husband to make use of the golem to remove the rock. She argued for hours, pointing out how many people could be helped with the gold. She so appealed to the rabbi's compassionate nature that he gave in and reluctantly promised to do what she was pleading for.

That night the rabbi and his wife did not sleep a wink. At dawn Rabbi Leib went up to the synagogue attic, engraved the Holy Name on the golem's forehead, and bade the golem remove the rock and dig out the gold where it was hidden.

Before, when the Rabbi gave an order to the golem, the golem said yes, and this was a sign of his willingness and his ability to do what he was told. But this time the golem did not answer. He sat up and stared at the rabbi in the moonlight that came through the crevices of the roof. There was something defiant in the golem's gaze. Rabbi Leib asked, "Did you hear what I ordered you to do?" And the golem said, "Yes."

"Will you do it?" Rabbi Leib asked. And the golem replied, "No."

"Why not?" Rabbi Leib asked in amazement. For a while the golem seemed to ponder, then he said, "Golem don't know." Rabbi Leib realized that he, the rabbi, had done wrong by giving in to Genendel. Such are the rules of all magic that the slightest misuse spoils its power. Since Rabbi Leib had promised the Emperor to end the golem's existence, he said to the golem, "Bend down your head." It was the rabbi's intention to erase the Holy Name from the golem's forehead once and forever. But, instead of bending down his head, the golem said, "No." It was clear to the rabbi that he had lost his authority over the golem for good.

The rabbi was grieved. There was no use arguing with a mindless golem. Rabbi Leib had made a mistake that he was unable to correct.

In the city of Prague the news spread both among Jews and among Christians that Rabbi Leib had lost his dominion over the golem, who was walking around in Rabbi Leib's courtyard, clumsily assisting Todrus the beadle. People expected the Emperor to punish Rabbi Leib and perhaps to bring harsh decrees on the whole Jewish community. It seemed, however, that even such a mighty Emperor as Rudolf II was hesitant to aggravate Rabbi Leib, the Jews, and especially the golem. Besides, the golem seemed not to be dangerous to anybody. He acted like an overgrown child, eager to serve people. Funny stories were told about him.

Usually a water carrier brought water to the house of Rabbi Leib to use for cooking and washing. It happened that the water carrier became sick and Genendel asked the golem to bring water to the house. He eagerly fetched two buckets and ran to the well. When the girls who came to the well to fetch water and wash linen saw the golem, they became frightened, left their own buckets or their linen, and ran off in terror. The golem filled up his buckets, carried them with great speed to the rabbi's kitchen, and poured the water into the water cistern. Genendel happened to leave the house for some household chore, and the golem brought water over and over again. When the rabbi's wife returned, all the rooms of the house were flooded. Genendel tried to explain to the golem that the water had to be filled to the top of the water cistern and no more, but this was impossible for the golem to grasp.

Until then, the golem never had any need for food. Suddenly he began to develop an appetite. When Genendel gave him a loaf of bread, he swallowed it at once. When he became thirsty, he put his face into a pail of water and drank half of it in one gulp. Once, when he went out and the children in the street were playing tag, he began to play with them, leaping and hurdling over everything in his path. Once when the golem entered the kitchen and the rabbi's cook was heating a full pot of meat, the golem grabbed the pot and poured it all into his mouth.

Since there was no way for Rabbi Leib to do away

with him, the rabbi decided to teach him to behave like a human being, but the golem's mentality was that of a one-year-old child, while his strength was that of a lion. He did not speak, but howled. When something pleased him, he laughed wildly. When something irritated him, he fell into an awful rage. Once, when Genendel gave him a bowl of soup with a spoon, he swallowed the spoon with the soup. Like a child, he considered everything a toy. He would lift up a horse and run with it. Once the golem passed a monument—a bronze king with a sword in his hand and mounted on a stallion. The golem became so excited that he tore the monument from its foundation and ran with it.

Everything was a plaything to him: a ladder, a pile of bricks, a barrel full of pickles, a living soldier. He would enter a bakery, shovel out all the loaves from the oven, and try to swallow them. Once he tried to eat all the meat in a butcher shop. At times, something good also developed from his antics. Once he passed a burning house where firemen were fighting the fire. The golem jumped into the house and extinguished the flames with his bare hands. When he came out, he was black with smoke and soot. The firemen hosed him down with water.

After a while he began to show some signs of maturity and spiritual growth. He seemed to be learning the Yiddish language better and uttered the words more clearly. He displayed some ability to develop and mature. Some Jews in Prague believed that it was worthwhile to bear all the golem's misdeeds, hoping that he might mature one day and become a constant defender of the Jews in Bohemia and perhaps in other countries as well. There were even some who thought that perhaps he was a forerunner of the Messiah. It was known that the enemies of the Jews were very disturbed by the existence of the golem, and felt threatened by him and by his might. There were fortunetellers in Prague who predicted that with the help of the golem the Jews would rule the whole world. However, Rabbi Leib did not share their hopes. He knew that our salvation could never come from sheer physical strength.

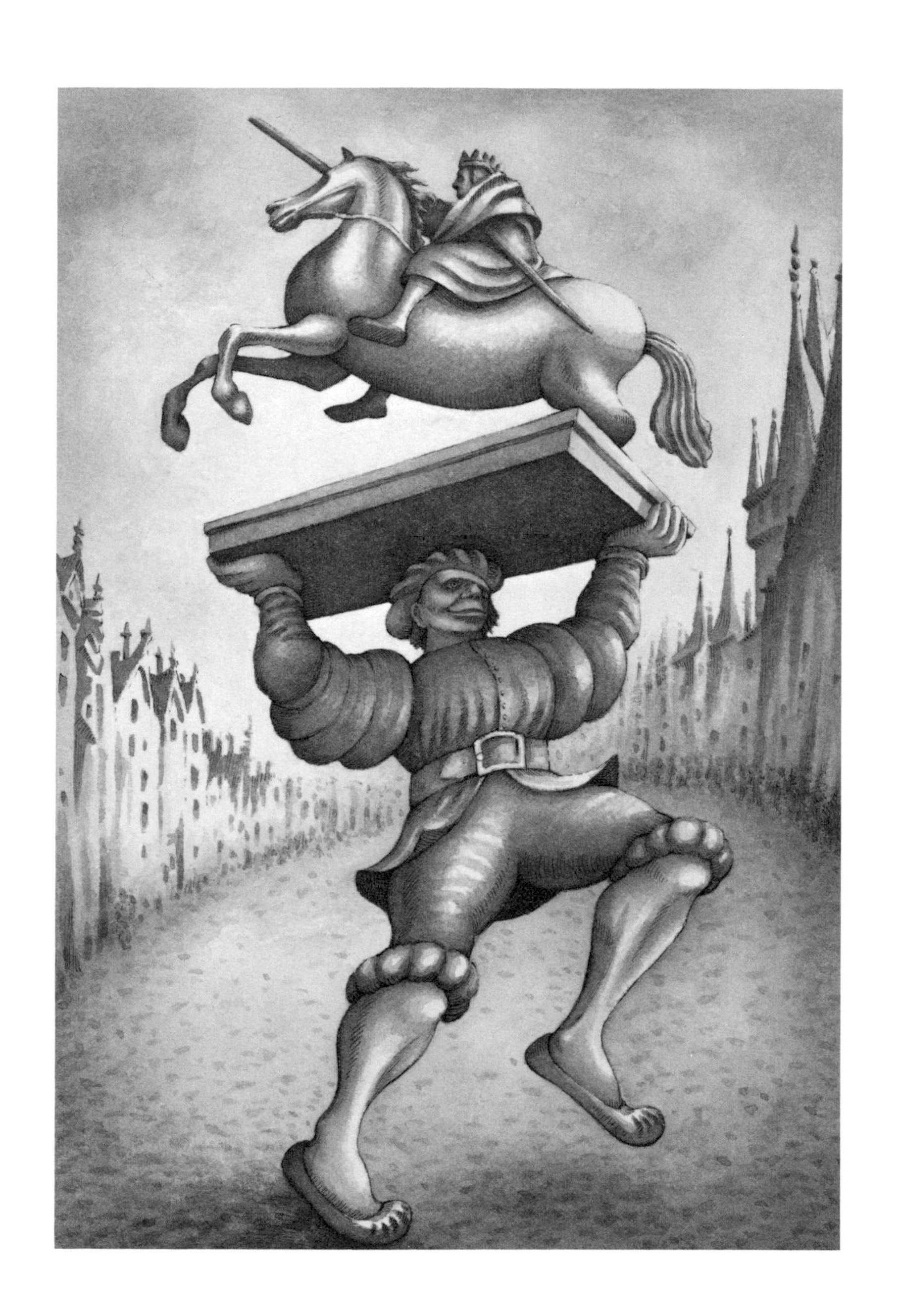

To his disappointment Rabbi Leib began to realize that the golem was becoming more human from day to day; he sneezed, he yawned, he laughed, he cried. He even developed a desire for clothes. Once, when Rabbi Leib fell asleep in the daytime, he woke up and saw the golem trying to put on his fur hat and his fringed garment and even his slippers, although none of them fit. He stood at the mirror and made faces. Rabbi Leib also noticed that the golem began to sprout a beard. Was the golem about to become a man like all other men?

Once, when Rabbi Leib sat in his study reading a book, the golem entered. Until then, the golem always barged in with noise and tumult. This time he opened the door carefully and came in with quiet steps. Rabbi Leib lifted his eyes from the book. "Joseph, what do you want?" he asked.

The golem did not answer immediately. He seemed to hesitate for a minute, and then he asked, "Who Golem?"

Rabbi Leib looked at him in bafflement.

"You are Joseph the golem."

"Golem old?"

"Not old."

"Golem Bar Mitzvah?"

Rabbi Leib could not believe his own ears. Where did the golem learn about such things?

"No, Joseph."

"Golem want Bar Mitzvah."

"You still have a lot of time."

The golem kept silence. Then he asked, "Who golem father?"

"The father of all of us is in heaven," Rabbi Leib answered.

"Who golem mother?"

"You have no mother."

"Golem brother, sister?"

"No, Joseph."

The golem winced. Suddenly he let out a harrowing cry. Rabbi Leib trembled. "Why do you cry, Joseph?"

"Golem alone."

A great feeling of compassion took hold of Rabbi

Leib. "Don't cry. You have helped the Jews, you have saved the whole community. Everybody is your friend."

The golem seemed to ponder these words. "Golem no want be golem," he cried out.

"What do you want to be?"

"Golem want father, mother. Everybody run from golem."

"I will let it be known in the synagogue on the Sabbath, before the reading of the Torah, that no one should ever run away from you. Now bend your head."

"No!"

Rabbi Leib bit his lips. "Joseph, you were not created like everybody. You have done your task, and now it is time for you to sleep. Bend your head, and I will put you to rest."

"Golem no want rest."

"What do you want?"

"Golem no want be golem," the golem cried out in a wailing voice.

Shocked by the golem's outcry, Rabbi Leib said, "Be good, Joseph, You fulfilled God's command.

When we need you, we will wake you. I implore you, bend your head."

"No!"

The golem left the study and slammed the door. He began to run through the streets of Prague, and whoever saw him was seized with fright. The golem stepped on a basket of fruit and broke the stalls of vegetable vendors. He overturned barrels and boxes. Rabbi Leib heard what was going on, and he prayed to God that the golem would not do anything that would disgrace the community. It wasn't long before a high police officer entered the rabbi's study. He said, "Rabbi, your golem is destroying the city. You will have to curb him. If not, all the Jews will have to leave the city of Prague."

The government was not satisfied with warning Rabbi Leib. An order went out to seize the golem, bind him in chains, and if he put up resistance, chop off his head. Some of the streets that led to the palace were blocked off. Here and there, ditches were dug so that the golem would fall into them if he passed that way. But the golem was afraid neither of soldiers nor of fences nor of ditches. He hurdled all the

barriers. He caught living soldiers and began to play with them as if they were lead toys. Heavy stones bounced off him as if he were made of steel. After a while he returned to the ghetto. He passed a cheder where a teacher was teaching little children the alphabet. The golem went into the cheder and sat on a bench. The children gazed with astonishment at the giant who sat down among them. Even in a sitting position, his head reached the ceiling. The teacher realized that the best thing to do was continue teaching as if nothing had happened. "Aleph, Bet, Gimmel, Daled . . ." he recited and pointed with a wooden pointer to the letters he had written down on a tablet.

"Aleph, Bet, Gimmel, Daled," the golem repeated with a voice that made the walls shake.

Todrus the beadle appeared at the open door. "Joseph, the rabbi wants to see you."

"Golem want Aleph, Bet, Gimmel, Daled," the golem announced.

"You must come with me," Todrus said.

For a moment the golem looked enraged. It seemed that he was about to catch Todrus with his huge paws and break every bone in his body. However, he soon rose and left with Todrus. When they arrived at the rabbi's study, it was already twilight. Rabbi Leib had gone to the synagogue for the evening prayers. The golem went into the kitchen. An oil lamp was burning. The rabbi's wife, Genendel, was praying from a prayer book. All of the rabbi's children were married and had children of their own. Besides her maid, Genendel kept an orphan girl named Miriam, who helped with the household chores. The golem sat down on the floor. He seemed to be tired. Miriam asked, "Joseph, are you hungry?"

"Hungry," the golem repeated.

Miriam brought him a large bowl of grits, and the golem finished it off at once. Then he said, "Golem hungry."

Miriam brought him bread, onions, and radishes. The golem gulped them all down in no time. Miriam smiled. She asked, "Where do you put all this food?"

"Food," the golem echoed. Suddenly he said, "Miriam nice girl."

Miriam began to laugh. "Hey, golem, I didn't know that you notice girls."

"Miriam nice girl," the golem said.

If another man had said this to Miriam, she would have gotten red in the face. In those times girls were known to be shy. But, before a golem, Miriam felt no embarrassment. She asked playfully. "Would you want me for a bride?"

"Yes, bride." He gazed at her with large eyes. Suddenly he did something that startled Miriam. He lifted her up and kissed her. His lips were as scratchy as a horseradish grinder. Miriam screamed and the golem exclaimed, "Miriam golem bride." He put her down and clapped his huge hands. Just then, Genendel entered, and Miriam told her what had happened.

The day after, Rabbi Leib called Miriam to his study and made her promise that at the first opportunity when the golem bent his head she would erase the Holy Name on his forehead. The rabbi told her that there would be no sin in this, because the golem was not a human being but only an artificial and temporary creature. The rabbi explained to her that the golem had no soul, only a nefesh—the kind of spirit that is given to higher animals.

Miriam promised the rabbi to do as she was told. However, days passed, and although the golem often bent down his head to her, somehow she was unable to erase the Holy Name from his head. Meanwhile, the golem kept doing one wild thing after another. One day, when he passed by the Tower of Five and noticed the watchman above circling the huge bell, the golem began to clamber up the tower with the agility of an ape. In a matter of minutes he had reached the balcony on top. When the watchman saw the golem scaling the walls of the tower, he was so alarmed that he began to ring the bell. A multitude of people gathered to see the golem's performance. Soldiers and firemen heard the alarm and came rushing. Once at the top, the golem pushed the watchman through the doorway that led to the spiral steps, and he began circling the bell with great speed. It was some time before the golem got tired of this game, and then he slid down the tower wall in a few seconds. He seemed to have the eyes of an eagle, because when he spotted Miriam in the crowd, he rushed over to her, caught her in his arms, and ran cheerfully with her through the streets, jumping and dancing with joy. When Rabbi Leib learned what the golem had done, he reproached him bitterly for rousing the wrath of the people by his conduct. But the golem said, "Golem no bad. Golem nice."

The next day a carriage harnessed to eight white horses, with ten dragoons riding in front blowing horns and clearing the way, entered the ghetto gate. The carriage stopped at Rabbi Leib's house, and a general who served as the chief of the military alighted. Rabbi Leib came out to receive the great lord and bowed his head low. The general said, "I have come to you with an order from the Emperor."

"What is the order, Your Highness?"

"It was decreed by His Majesty that the golem be drafted into the army of Bohemia," the general said. "We will forge special weapons for him and teach him how to use them. We are giving your golem eight days to prepare for the service."

"But, Your Honor, the golem is not a man of flesh and blood," Rabbi Leib protested. "One cannot rely on him."

"We will teach him to become a warrior. With a soldier like the golem, we could subdue many of our enemies."

"Your Excellency, the golem was not created to wage war."

"Rabbi, I cannot go into details with you," the general said. "In eight days your golem will be a soldier. It is a royal decree." And the general returned to the carriage and left with his entourage.

Rabbi Leib began to pace back and forth. A deep sadness overtook him. He had created the golem to help the Jews. Now the golem was to become the Emperor's soldier. Who knows, he might attack his superiors and the Jews would be found responsible for his breach of discipline. Rabbi Leib called Miriam and said to her, "Miriam, you must somehow erase the Holy Name and do away with our golem. It cannot be delayed."

"Rabbi, I can't do it."

"Miriam, in the name of the Torah I order you to do it. I'm far from being a murderer, but clay must return to clay."

"Rabbi, I feel as if you had told me to kill a man."

"Miriam, I am ready to erase the Holy Name myself, but you will have to make him bend his head, or get him to fall asleep."

After a while Miriam said, "Rabbi, I will do what I can."

Miriam returned to the kitchen. The golem looked at her with wild eyes and shouted, "Golem hungry!"

Miriam opened the pantry, and he ate all the food in sight. He saw a bottle on the lowest shelf, grabbed it, and tried to swallow it.

"Joseph, what are you doing? Wait a second."

"What this?" the golem asked.

"Wine," Miriam said. "This is not to eat but to drink."

"Golem want wine."

Miriam filled a glass of wine for him and the golem swallowed it. She brought another bottle, and a third one, and the golem kept on drinking and calling, "More!" He was not yet drunk, and Miriam remembered that in his cellar the rabbi kept wine for the benediction on Sabbath, as well as Passover wine that the family drank at the Seder when everyone must drink four goblets of wine. "Joseph, let's go to the cellar," Miriam said. "There's a lot of wine there."

Miriam went down the steps into the cellar, and the golem followed her. It was cold in the cellar, and dark, but Miriam left the door open to the kitchen and some light streamed in. Rabbi Leib had heard what was going on and he stood at the door to the cellar to make sure the golem did not harm Miriam. Miriam said to the golem, "Now you can drink as much as you desire." As she said these words, she burst out crying. The golem snatched a barrel of wine, forced the stopper out, and began to drink. Miriam stood there gaping and choking on her tears. The golem kept gorging on the wine, breathing heavily and grunting from pleasure. The golem's eyes became both soft and savage. He cried out, "Golem love wine."

These were his last words. He fell down on the floor and started to snore. Rabbi Leib saw and heard what had happened and descended the stairs. He bent down over the golem and recited, "Earth to earth and dust to dust. God, blessed be He, is perfect, all His ways are judgment, a God of truth and without iniquity, just and right is He." After reciting these words, Rabbi Leib erased the Holy Name from the golem's forehead. He kissed the clay where the Holy Name was engraved. The golem gave one last snore and became lifeless.

Rabbi Leib went up to his study, but Miriam remained in the cellar. She bent down and kissed the golem's eyes and his mouth. She was crying so hard that her tears almost blinded her.

That night Rabbi Leib and Todrus carried the golem's body up to the attic of the synagogue. There was a great fear in the ghetto that when the Emperor learned that the golem was dead he might take revenge on all the Jews, especially Rabbi Leib. But it did not happen. For one thing, the military leaders were not happy about making the golem one of their own. They were afraid he might demoralize the whole service, or even attack his captains. It had also become clear to many Gentiles that the Jews were not as weak and helpless as their enemies thought they were. A great power was hidden in these people whom God had chosen for His own and whom He was bound to bring back to their glory at the End of Days.

Even though the golem was not a man, Rabbi Leib recited Kaddish for him.

Legends began to spread. The golem was seen at night in the Emperor's palace; he stood at a windmill turning its wings; he was seen standing at the top of the Tower of Five, his head in the clouds.

A startling event shook the ghetto: Miriam disappeared. One night Genendel saw her go to bed and heard her recite the "Shema" before falling asleep. The next morning her bed was empty. There were rumors that Miriam was seen at dawn walking toward the river, most probably to drown herself. Others believed that the golem was waiting for her in the darkness and took her with him to a place where loving spirits meet. Who knows? Perhaps love has even more power than a Holy Name. Love once engraved in the heart can never be erased. It lives forever.